Megafauna

Phillip Simpson

Contents

What Are Megafauna?

"Megafauna" is the name for the biggest animals that have ever lived. This word is made up of two smaller words: "mega", meaning big, and "fauna", meaning animals.

Most megafauna are very big and heavy. They can be plant-eaters or meat-eaters.

Some megafauna that live today are the elephant, the hippopotamus and the rhinoceros. The biggest megafauna lived during **prehistoric** times. They are now **extinct**.

rhinoceros

elephant

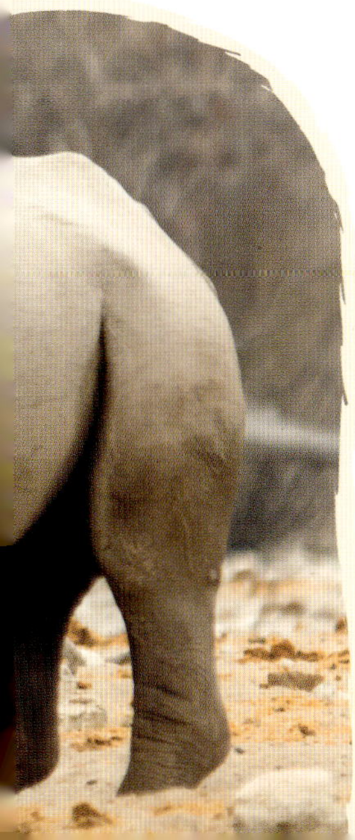

hippopotamus

Prehistoric megafauna lived thousands and thousands of years ago, in a time known as the **Ice Age**.

This is an artist's idea of what megafauna, like **woolly mammoths**, might have looked like during the Ice Age.

The last of the dinosaurs died out at the beginning of the Ice Age. Then, over many thousands of years, small mammals, birds and reptiles grew bigger and bigger. They became the prehistoric megafauna – the largest animals on Earth.

Scientists who study animal and plant **fossils** are called palaeontologists (say: *pay-lee-on-tol-o-jists*).

The largest prehistoric megafauna were plant-eaters. Palaeontologists believe that these mammals became so big because there were no dinosaurs left on Earth to eat the **vegetation**.

Meat-eating megafauna were not as big as the plant-eaters.
Their smaller size meant they could hide more easily to attack their prey.

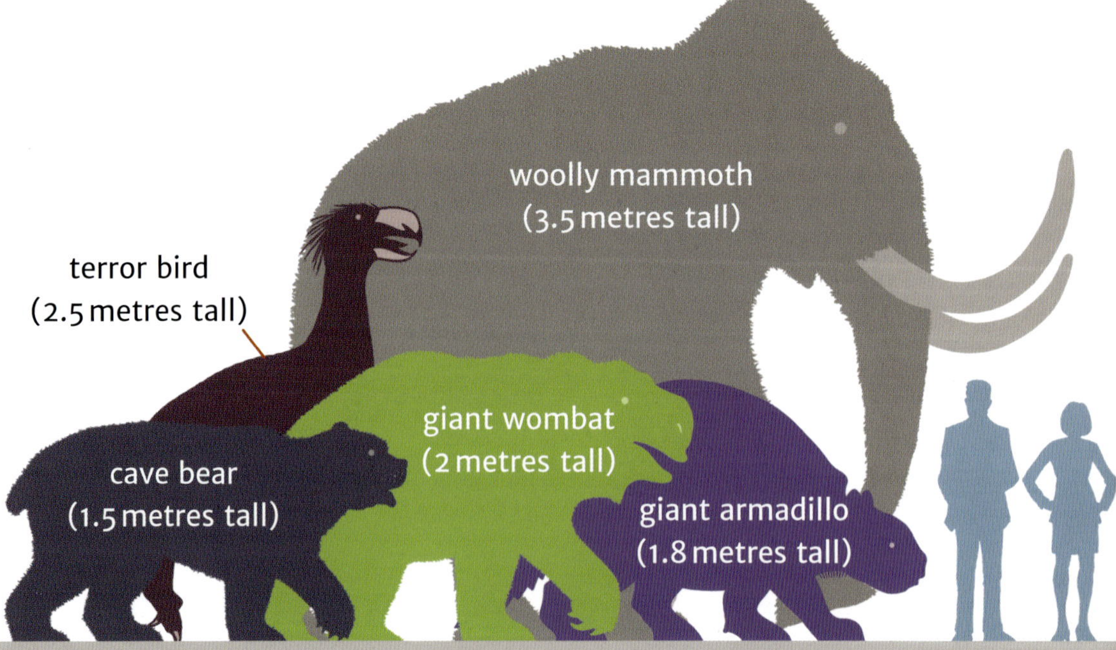

Compared to humans, prehistoric megafauna were very large.

Terror Bird

The terror bird was a giant meat-eating bird.
It lived on what is now the **continent** of North America.

The terror bird was about 2.5 metres tall
and could weigh up to 150 kilograms.

Scientists believe a terror bird looked something like this.

The terror bird had a solid body with a thick neck and a huge beak. It had a pair of wings, but it did not fly. Its wings were too small to carry its huge body into the air.

The terror bird had long legs, which palaeontologists believe made it a very fast runner.

The terror bird is thought to have been a fierce meat-eater that hunted other mammals.

Giant Armadillo

The giant armadillo was a kind of megafauna that lived during the Ice Age.
It looked like the giant armadillo that lives today, but it was much, much bigger.

It could grow to over 3 metres long and could weigh more than 1000 kilograms, or 1 tonne.

It had a solid shell that covered its whole body.
The shell was made up of hundreds of small scales, which helped to protect it from meat-eating predators.

The giant armadillo had a powerful tail, which it could swing at predators like a club.

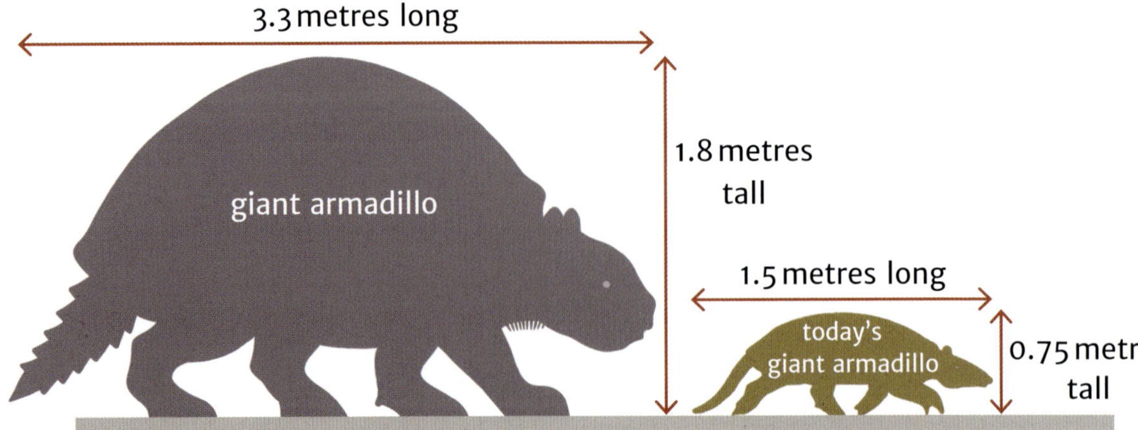

A giant armadillo exists today, but it is much smaller than the prehistoric giant armadillo.

This is an artist's idea of what the giant armadillo might have looked like.

Giant Wombat

The giant wombat lived on what is now the continent of Australia. This megafauna was about 3 metres long and 2 metres tall. It is thought to have weighed over 2000 kilograms.

The giant wombat had a heavy, square head. It looked a bit like a rhinoceros without a horn. It had strong claws on its front feet, which it used to clutch and grip plants. Like other **marsupials**, it had a pouch where its young could nestle.

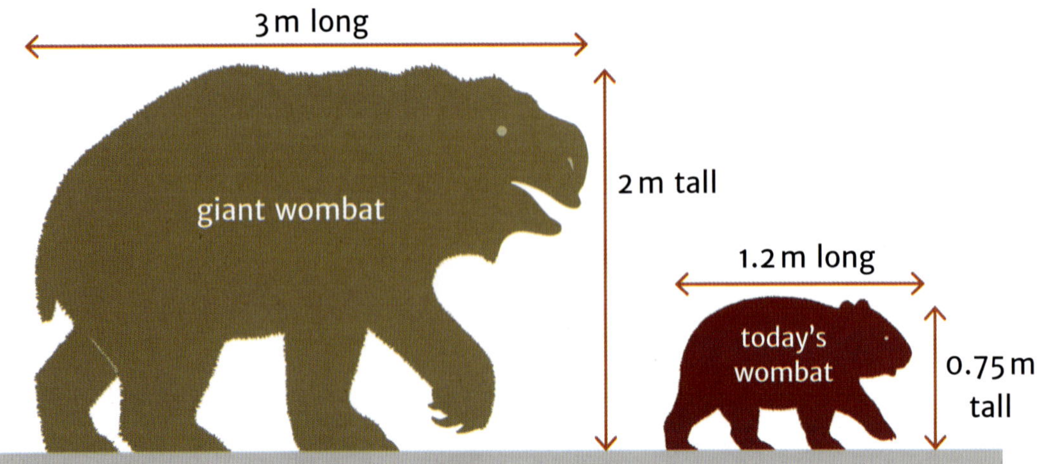

The giant wombat was nearly three times bigger than today's wombat.

Another name for the giant wombat is *Diprotodon* (say: *Die-pro-to-don*).

Cave Bear

The cave bear was a kind of giant bear.
It lived on what is now the continent of Europe.
It is known as the "cave bear" because most of its fossils have been found inside caves.

Scientists believe that the cave bear was probably the same size as a polar bear.

Despite its huge size, and its giant jaws and teeth, the cave bear mostly ate plants.

The cave bear mostly used its big teeth to eat plants.

Woolly Mammoth

Woolly mammoths are the most well known of the prehistoric megafauna.

Woolly mammoth fossils have been found in most places around the world, apart from Australia and South America.

Most woolly mammoths were the same size as elephants, but some types of mammoth were much larger. One of these was the Steppe mammoth. It was gigantic. It stood over 4 metres tall and weighed up to 10 tonnes.

Woolly mammoths had a thick layer of fat under their skin and a coat of long, dark-brown hair. These protected them from the cold.

Palaeontologists have found the bodies of woolly mammoths frozen in ice or in the ground.

Inside some of the bodies were spears and arrows. This proves that woolly mammoths were once hunted by humans.

Parts of human tools were found with this woolly mammoth fossil in France.

What Happened to the Prehistoric Megafauna?

Over 100 000 years ago, many prehistoric megafauna started to die out. Some scientists believe most megafauna became extinct because they were big and slow, and humans could easily hunt and kill them.

Some rock art shows how humans hunted megafauna.

This **ancient** rock art in England shows humans hunting big animals.

Other scientists believe that prehistoric megafauna became extinct because of **climate change**. Climate change is when the weather patterns on Earth change over time.

Megafauna and other animals struggled to survive at the end of the Ice Age.

As Earth became hotter at the end of the Ice Age, many megafauna did not survive.

Prehistoric megafauna walked Earth long after the dinosaurs. These magnificent animals were much larger than most of the animals alive now.

Today, palaeontologists can tell what megafauna may have looked like from their fossils.

Megafauna probably became extinct because of humans or climate change.

This giant wombat's skeleton gives scientists an idea of what it might have looked like.

Glossary

ancient (*adjective*) very old

climate change (*noun*) a change in weather patterns around the world

continent (*noun*) a very large area of land, usually made up of several countries

extinct (*adjective*) when a type of animal is gone forever

fossils (*noun*) what is left of something that lived a long time ago

Ice Age (*proper noun*) a time when Earth was mostly covered in ice

woolly mammoths (*noun*) hairy animals that looked like elephants

marsupials (*noun*) mammals that carry their babies in their pouches

prehistoric (*adjective*) from the time before written records, or history

vegetation (*noun*) the plants growing in an area

Index